# NORMAN THORMAN
### AND THE
# TOWERING TARANTULA
#### OF **TORREMOLINOS**

*by*

## LORNA KENT

*Illustrated by the author*

ARACHNID

HAMISH HAMILTON

LONDON

*For my mother*

## HAMISH HAMILTON LTD

Published by the Penguin Group
27 Wrights Lane, London w8 5tz, England
Penguin Books USA Inc., 375 Hudson Street, New York, New York 10014, USA
Penguin Books Australia Ltd, Ringwood, Victoria, Australia
Penguin Books Canada Ltd, 10 Alcorn Avenue, Toronto, Ontario, Canada m4v 3b2
Penguin Books (NZ) Ltd, 182–190 Wairau Road, Auckland 10, New Zealand

Penguin Books Ltd, Registered Offices: Harmondsworth, Middlesex, England

First published in Great Britain 1993 by Hamish Hamilton Ltd

British Library Cataloguing in Publication Data
CIP data for this book is available from the British Library

isbn 0-241-13356-4

Set in 15pt Baskerville by Rowland Phototypesetting Ltd
Bury St Edmunds, Suffolk
Printed in Great Britain by BPCC Hazell Books Ltd
Member of BPCC Ltd, Aylesbury, Bucks.

## Chapter One

Schoolboy Norman Thorman was on his way home from the trip of a lifetime. He had spent the whole of the school holidays staying with his uncle and aunt in the Spanish seaside resort of Torremolinos. Norman sat back in his aeroplane seat and thought about all the adventures they had had together. But little did he know that the biggest adventure was about to begin.

It all started when he got back home. As he unpacked his bag, a tiny spider that had been hiding in a rolled-up sock decided to make its escape.

"You're a long way from home," said Norman, picking it up gently. "I'm afraid you'll have to live with me now."

The spider ran around Norman's palm for a few moments and then disappeared up his sleeve.

"Hey, come back!" cried Norman. He felt the spider run across his chest, over his shoulder and down his back. "Stop it, you're tickling me," he laughed.

As Norman thrashed about trying to catch his new pet, he lost his balance and crashed into his desk. He ended up on the floor covered in the chemistry experiment he had set up before the holidays.

"Oh no!" groaned Norman. "That's the end of my miracle hair restorer experiment. Only one more week and it would have been ready."

He rescued the spider from a pool of liquid, popped it into his bug bottle and wrote ARACHNID on the label.

"I think I'll call you Tarquin," said Norman as he hid the bug bottle under his bed. "We can't have Mum and Dad finding you. They don't like spiders."

That night Norman tossed and turned and had some really strange dreams. The next morning he ate his breakfast in a daze.

"Oh Norman, you're not even dressed yet," snapped Mrs Thorman. "And what's the matter with your hair? What have you done to it?"

"Nothing," yawned Norman as he wandered off to get ready for school.

"Well, it's too late to do anything with it now," flapped Mrs Thorman. "Honestly, Norman, sometimes I'd swear your hair grows inches overnight. I think we'll take a trip to the hairdresser's after school."

## Chapter Two

The first lesson that morning was football.

"What's the matter with your hair, boy!" bellowed Mr Fitt, the games teacher. "Why is it sticking up in the air like that?"

"I don't know, sir," replied Norman, reaching up to feel his hair. It certainly didn't feel normal. It felt as if he'd washed it in glue, which of course he hadn't.

"You surprise me, Norman!" sighed Mr Fitt. "You should pay more attention to your appearance, especially as you are the Register Monitor."

"I didn't do it on purpose," explained Norman, but Mr Fitt wasn't listening.

As Norman changed into his football kit he kept trying to flatten his hair down, but it was no use. The harder he tried the stiffer and spikier it became. All Norman's friends were amazed. They thought it was a brilliant hairstyle. That was until it got so spiky it burst three footballs and Norman was sent off.

"Whatever it is you've put on your

hair, I want it washed off immediately!" demanded Mr Fitt.

Norman washed his hair but it made no difference. He began to think it was one of his dad's practical jokes. "He could have put glue in the shampoo bottle . . . No, even Dad wouldn't do that."

Norman sat in the changing room waiting for the game to finish. He was so busy reading his book that he didn't notice what was happening to his hair. Slowly it grew about six inches, pointing straight up in the air. Then the whole lot began to twist into a stiff peak on top of his head.

After Norman heard the final whistle he ran outside to see what

the score was.

When Mr Fitt saw Norman's hair he was so shocked, he walked straight into the goal post and almost knocked himself out!

"What the? . . . How? . . . Why? . . . " he gasped. "I shall be writing to your parents for an explanation!"

At lunch Norman was really fed up. What was causing his hair to behave so strangely?

"At least things can't get any worse," he thought. But they did . . . The dreaded hair jokes started.

"Where does Norman Thorman live?"

"In a block of PLAITS!"

"What's Norman Thorman's favourite way of travelling?"

"By HAIROPLANE!"

"What does Norman Thorman eat at tea time?"

"Currant BUNS!"

Norman was relieved when school was over. As soon as the bell went he dashed off to meet his mum at the school gate.

"Good grief!" shrieked Mrs Thorman when she saw Norman's hair. "You look like a unicorn!"

"Come on, Mum," said Norman, pulling his stunned mother through the school gates. "Let's go and get my hair cut before I hear any more corny jokes."

At Baldycoot's Unisex Hair Salon, the hairdresser shook her head. "There's something very wrong here," she said, inspecting her bent and twisted scissors. "Norman's hair is so strong I can't cut it!"

"That does it!" exclaimed Mrs Thorman. "I'm taking you straight to the hospital."

The Thorman's were well known at the hospital, as this wasn't the first time that something weird had happened to Norman.

"Hello, Norman," said the doctor. "And how do you feel today?"

"I feel stupid," muttered Norman.

"He's a little sensitive at the moment," explained Mrs Thorman. "He's had a bad day at school."

Mrs Thorman whisked the paper bag off Norman's head. "What do you think, Doctor?" she asked.

"Well I never!" exclaimed the doctor, staring at Norman's hair. "You really are full of surprises."

"I suppose this means lots of tests," said Mrs Thorman.

"I'm afraid it does," replied the doctor. "But don't worry, I don't think it's serious."

"Huh, that's easy for you to say," said Norman. "How can I be a Register Monitor with hair like this?"

Mrs Thorman left Norman with the doctor and went off to phone her husband at work. "This is not going to be easy to explain," she thought.

That evening Mr and Mrs Thorman
sat in the hospital waiting room
while Norman was being examined.
Mrs Thorman wondered if the new
brand of shampoo she'd bought
recently could be responsible for
Norman's condition.

Norman and the doctor eventually
emerged.

"Well, apart from his hair growing
in a most unusual manner, your son
appears to be in perfect health," said
the doctor. "We shall be sending
samples to a specialist for further
investigation. And don't worry, we'll
soon get to the ROOT of the
problem."

"Oh no!" thought Norman. "Not
*more* hair jokes."

It was quite dark when the Thormans got home. Norman was the first to notice something was very wrong.

"What's my bed doing on the front lawn?" he gasped.

"What on earth? . . . " began Mr Thorman.

"Look!" screamed Mrs Thorman, pointing up to the huge hole in the side of the house.

"That's my bedroom!" shrieked Norman.

"I just knew that chemistry set would lead to trouble," cried Mrs Thorman.

"Oh Norman, you really are the limit," snapped Mr Thorman.

Norman began to protest. "But

I haven't . . . It wasn't . . . I didn't . . . " But it was useless. Mr Thorman was busy trying to cover the hole with plastic sheeting while Mrs Thorman phoned the builder.

As Norman picked up the rest of his belongings that were scattered on the lawn he saw his bug bottle in pieces on the path. "Poor little Tarquin, he didn't stand a chance."

## Chapter Three

Norman spent a comfortable night
on the sofa and woke feeling
refreshed. He jumped out of bed and
ran into the kitchen for breakfast.
The look of astonishment on his
mum and dad's face soon reminded
him of his problem. His hair had
grown even longer and was sticking
out of his head in big spikes.

"Stop looking at me like that,"

snapped Norman, feeling his head. "I can't help it."

"I'm sorry, son," grinned Mr Thorman. "It's just that you remind me of someone . . . something . . ."

"George!" warned Mrs Thorman.

"I know what it is!" laughed Mr Thorman. "You look like the Statue of Liberty!"

Even Mrs Thorman began to laugh. "Don't mind us," she smiled.

"It's just that we're not used to seeing you like this."

Norman groaned. "Try not to worry, darling," said Mrs Thorman. "I'm sure you'll be back to normal soon."

"Yes," said Mr Thorman. "As the old saying goes: HAIR today, gone tomorrow!"

"It's not funny!" shouted Norman. "I don't know what it's going to do next!"

After lunch Mr Thorman hid himself behind a large newspaper. This was partly because he was interested in the news and partly to stop himself laughing at Norman's hair.

"Good grief!" cried Mr Thorman,

suddenly sitting bolt upright. "How extraordinary!" he exclaimed, pointing to the newspaper.

"Town in Towering Tarantula Terror! . . . Traffic was brought to a standstill today as a giant tarantula, with a body the size of a very large elephant, made its way through the town towards the shopping centre. A government spokesman who was at the scene said . . . 'We do not yet know how the tarantula came to be in this country or why it has grown to such an enormous size. We have a theory that a strange chemical reaction has taken place and we have a team of top government scientists working on it at this very moment. The public are strongly urged to stay at home until we have the creature under control.'"

"Well I suppose it had to happen one day, what with all that chemical rubbish they spray on the fields these days," sighed Mr Thorman. "At least nobody interferes with our vegetable plot."

"They did once," said Norman, remembering an incident involving marrows. But that's another story.

Suddenly there was an urgent knock at the door. "Oh no!" gasped Norman as he rushed upstairs to his bedroom. "I don't want anyone to see me like this."

"Hello, I'm from Mars," said the man on the doorstep.

"Yes and I'm the Queen of

England," replied Mr Thorman, quickly closing the door.

"Who was it, dear?" asked Mrs Thorman.

"Oh, just a mad man who claims he's from Mars," replied Mr Thorman.

"Poor chap should be in a hospital," said Mrs Thorman.

"Hello . . . hello," called the voice through the letterbox. "I'm Professor Fly from M.A.R.S. The Mutant Arachnid Recovery Service. I must speak to your son Norman!"

"Oh no," groaned an embarrassed Mr Thorman as he rushed to open the door. "I'm sorry about that," he apologized. "I thought you were a bit umm . . . err . . . Do come in."

"Would you like a cup of tea?"
asked Mrs Thorman.

"I'm afraid there's no time for
tea," explained Professor Fly. "The
hospital has informed me that
Norman's tests reveal a strange
unknown chemical also present in
the hairs from a gigantic tarantula!"

Norman had been sitting at the
top of the stairs and had heard
everything. He thought about the
spider he had accidently brought
back from Torremolinos, the

chemistry experiment, his weird hair, the huge hole in his bedroom wall and the broken bug bottle on the path. Suddenly everything became clear.

"Oh no!" he gasped. "The giant tarantula must be Tarquin! He probably ate some of my experimental hair restorer when it fell on us. That would also explain why my hair is behaving so strangely. Tarquin must have crashed through my bedroom wall when he grew too big!"

Suddenly a local news flash appeared on the television. Norman could just see it from the top of the stairs.

"At this very moment the town

centre is being held in a vice-like grip of terror. A terrifying giant tarantula is towering over the shopping centre. The creature has doubled in size since it was discovered in the early hours of this morning and is continuing to grow rapidly." The camera zoomed in for a close up shot of the tarantula.

"It *is* Tarquin!" thought Norman. "I recognize him!"

The newsflash continued . . . "The emergency services are at the scene, but surely it's only a matter of time before something dreadful happens. This is Roger Roving reporting for Channel Four."

"It's not Tarquin's fault," thought Norman. "He doesn't want to hurt anyone. He may be huge but he's still only a baby."

Norman felt terrible. "It's all my fault," he said. "I've got do something!"

He wasn't sure what he could do but he knew he had to act fast! He ran into his bedroom and locked the door behind him. Then he grabbed his chemistry set, opened the window and climbed down the drainpipe.

"I hope Mum and Dad don't notice I've gone for a while," thought Norman as he jumped on his bike and sped off towards the shopping centre.

## Chapter Four

When Norman reached the town
centre it was chaos. He soon spotted
who was in charge of the situation. It
was a large man with a loud voice
wearing an army uniform covered in
stripes and medals. Norman took his
Register Monitor's badge from his
pocket and pinned it to his jumper
before introducing himself.

"Norman Thorman reporting for

duty, sir!" saluted Norman.

General Boom was not easily shocked but the sight of Norman's spiky, helmet-like hair left him speechless for a few seconds.

Norman explained all about Tarquin and the failed hair restorer experiment. "He doesn't want to hurt anyone," he said. "He's only a baby really."

"He may not want to hurt anyone," said General Boom, "but it's extremely inconvenient for him to be sitting in the middle of the shopping centre. There are a lot of people who don't take kindly to spiders."

"You can say that again!" said an irate shopkeeper. "Nobody can get in or out of my shop with that great big lump sitting in the way!"

"He's not a lump," protested Norman. "He's a tarantula. And he's just as upset as everyone else."

"The situation has become critical, Norman," explained the General. "The tarantula has now become so big, it's stuck between Macdougal's hamburger restaurant and Woolco's supermarket. If it gets any bigger or if it tries to move it will knock the buildings down."

"I've got to do something now or it will be too late," thought Norman.

Norman waited until General Boom was busy giving orders, then he tucked his chemistry set up his jumper and ran towards

Macdougal's, jumping over bags of shopping that had been dropped in the panic. Eventually he entered the back door of Macdougal's and found himself in the kitchen. When he saw all the hamburgers he had a brainwave. Without a moments hesitation he piled them all onto a big tray and took the lift to the top floor. When he was about half way up, the lift began to shake. "Oh no!" thought Norman. "Tarquin's getting restless, I must hurry!"

The lift doors opened and Norman bounded up the last few stairs and out onto the roof.

Suddenly he was face to face with Tarquin, whose big, sad eyes were filled with confusion.

"Don't worry, Tarquin!" called Norman. "I got you into this mess and now I'm going to get you out!"

Then Norman whipped out his chemistry set and started to mix up all kinds of chemical concoctions. One by one he smeared the hamburgers with the different experimental antidotes.

"I'm sorry I have to experiment on you," said Norman. "But this is an emergency."

Tarquin was very hungry and soon wolfed his way through most of the hamburgers. Unfortunately nothing seemed to be working.

"Only one hamburger left," sighed Norman. "This is our last chance."

Just then Norman's concentration was shattered by the screeching of car brakes down below. Three people jumped out of the car and ran towards Macdougal's.

"Norman! Norman!" shouted the woman. "Come down from that building at once!"

"I'm coming up to get you, Norman," shouted the man. "Stay away from the edge!"

"Oh no!" gasped Norman, recognising the voices. "It's Mum and Dad with Professor Fly. I need more time to mix the last potion."

Norman furiously mixed the last of the chemicals together and spread them on the last burger. Tarquin swallowed it in one gulp as Norman sank to the floor exhausted. "I'm sorry, Tarquin," he sighed. "There's nothing more I can do now."

After about a minute Norman noticed a strange look in Tarquin's eyes. Gradually the creature began to shrink. Slowly at first and then quite quickly. "I've done it! I've done it!" shrieked Norman, jumping up and down. "I've discovered the antidote."

In only ten minutes Tarquin had shrunk to his original size. Professor Fly quickly put him in his super-secure unbreakable bug box.

Everyone cheered and clapped as Norman hugged his parents. "Well done, Norman!" boomed General Boom. "If you want a career in the army you've only got to ask, I'm sure something could be done about that hair."

"Thank you," replied Norman.
"But I've already got a very
important job as a Register
Monitor."

"You're a genius, Norman!" beamed Professor Fly. "How did you work out the antidote formula so quickly?"

"In my job I'm expected to know a lot of things," said Norman, proudly polishing his Register Monitor's badge on his sleeve.

Fortunately Mr and Mrs Thorman were so thankful that Norman was safe they forgot to tell him off, which was a relief for Norman.

"What will happen to Tarquin now?" asked Norman.

"We'll keep him under observation at MARS for a while," replied Professor Fly. "Just to make sure he doesn't start growing again. Then we will send him back home."

Norman was quite sad to say goodbye to Tarquin, but he knew it was for the best.

The antidote took a little longer to work on Norman. It wasn't until later that evening at dinner, that his hair collapsed into his soup.

"We could have been rich if my miracle hair restorer experiment had worked," Norman told his parents. "Maybe with a bit more work I could . . ."

"I think you've done quite enough experimenting, dear," said Mrs Thorman.

"Never mind," said Mr Thorman. "You may not be the inventor of a miracle hair restorer, but there's one thing you'll always be."

"What's that?" asked Norman, expecting the worst.

"Our HAIRO."

And, of course, everyone groaned.